Circe's Palace

Nathaniel Hawthorne

Some of you have heard no doubt, of the wise King Ulysses, and how he went to the siege of Troy, and how, after that famous city was taken and burned, he spent ten long years in trying to get back again to his own little kingdom of Ithaca. At one time in the course of this weary voyage, he arrived at an island that looked very green and pleasant, but the name of which was unknown to him. For, only a little while before he came thither, he had met with a terrible hurricane, or rather a great many hurricanes at once, which drove his fleet of vessels into a strange part of the sea, where neither himself nor any of his mariners had ever sailed. This misfortune was entirely owing to the foolish curiosity of his ship-mates, who, while Ulysses lay asleep, had untied some very bulky leathern bags, in which they supposed a valuable treasure to be concealed. But in each of these stout bags, King Æolus, the ruler of the winds, had tied up a tempest, and had given it to Ulysses to keep, in order that he might be sure of a favorable passage homeward to Ithaca; and when the strings were loosened, forth rushed the whistling blasts, like air out of a blown bladder, whitening the sea with foam, and scattering the vessels nobody could tell whither.

Immediately after escaping from this peril, a still greater one had befallen him. Scudding before the hurricane, he reached a place, which, as he afterwards found, was called Læstrygonia, where some monstrous giants had eaten up many of his companions, and had sunk every one of his vessels, except that in which he himself sailed, by flinging great masses of rock at them, from the cliffs along the shore. After going through such troubles as these, you cannot wonder that King Ulysses was glad to moor his tempest-beaten bark in a quiet cove of the green island, which I began with telling you about. But he had encountered so many dangers from giants, and one-eyed Cyclopes, and monsters of the sea and land, that he could not help dreading some mischief, even in this pleasant and seemingly solitary spot. For two days, therefore, the poor weatherworn voyagers kept quiet, and either staid on board of their vessel, or merely crept along under the cliffs that bordered the shore; and to keep themselves alive, they dug shellfish out of the sand, and sought for any little rill of fresh water that might be running towards the sea.

Before the two days were spent, they grew very weary of this kind of life; for the followers of King Ulysses, as you will find it important to remember, were terrible gormandizers, and pretty sure to grumble if they missed their regular meals, and their irregular ones besides. Their stock of provisions was quite exhausted, and even the shellfish began to get scarce, so that they had now to choose between starving to death or venturing into the interior of the island, where perhaps some huge three-headed dragon, or other horrible monster, had his den. Such misshapen creatures were very numerous in those days; and nobody ever expected to make a voyage, or take a journey, without running more or less risk of being devoured by them.

But King Ulysses was a bold man as well as a prudent one; and on the third morning he determined to discover what sort of a place the island was, and whether it were possible to obtain a supply of food for the hungry mouths of his companions. So, taking a spear in his hand, he clambered to the summit of a cliff and gazed round about him. At a distance, towards the center of the island, he beheld the stately towers of what seemed to be a palace, built of snow-white marble, and rising in the midst of a grove of lofty trees. The thick branches of these trees stretched across the front of the edifice, and more than half concealed it, although, from the portion which he saw, Ulysses judged it to be spacious and exceedingly beautiful, and probably the residence of some great nobleman or prince. A blue smoke went curling up from the chimney, and was almost the pleasantest part of the spectacle to Ulysses. For, from the abundance of this smoke, it was reasonable to conclude that there was a good fire in the kitchen, and that, at dinner time, a plentiful banquet would be served up to the inhabitants of the palace, and to whatever guests might happen to drop in.

With so agreeable a prospect before him, Ulysses fancied that he could not do better than to go straight to the palace gate, and tell the master of it that there was a crew of poor ship-wrecked mariners not far off, who had eaten nothing for a day or two, save a few clams and oysters, and would therefore be thankful for a little food. And the prince or nobleman must be a very stingy curmudgeon, to be sure, if, at least, when his own dinner was over, he would not bid them welcome to the broken victuals from the table.

Pleasing himself with this idea, King Ulysses had made a few steps in the direction of the palace, when there was a great twittering and chirping from the branch of a neighboring tree. A moment afterwards, a bird came flying towards him, and hovered in the air, so as almost to brush his face with its wings. It was a very pretty little bird, with purple wings and body, and yellow legs, and a circle of golden feathers round its neck, and on its head a golden tuft, which looked like a king's crown in miniature. Ulysses tried to catch the bird. But it fluttered nimbly out of his reach, still chirping in a piteous tone, as if it could have told a lamentable story, had it only been gifted with human language. And when he attempted to drive it away, the bird flew no farther than the bough of the next tree, and again came fluttering about his head, with its doleful chirp, as soon as he showed a purpose of going forward.

"Have you anything to tell me, little bird?" asked Ulysses.

And he was ready to listen attentively to whatever the bird might communicate; for, at the siege of Troy, and elsewhere, he had known such odd things to happen, that he would not have considered it much out of the common run had this little feathered creature talked as plainly as himself.

"Peep!" said the bird, "peep, peep, pe—weep!" And nothing else would it say, but only, "Peep, peep, pe—weep!" in a melancholy cadence, and over and over and over again. As often as Ulysses moved forward, however, the bird showed the greatest alarm, and did its best to drive him back, with the anxious flutter of its purple wings. Its unaccountable behavior made him conclude, at last, that the bird knew of some danger that awaited him, and which must needs be very terrible, beyond all question, since it moved even a little fowl to feel compassion for a human being. So he resolved, for the present, to return to the vessel, and tell his companions what he had seen. This appeared to satisfy the bird. As soon as Ulysses turned back, it ran up the trunk of a tree, and began to pick insects out of the bark with its long, sharp bill; for it was a kind of woodpecker, you must know, and had to get its living in the same manner as other birds of that species. But every little while, as it pecked at the bark of the tree, the purple bird bethought itself of some secret sorrow, and repeated its plaintive note of "Peep, peep, pe—weep!"

On his way to the shore, Ulysses had the good luck to kill a large stag by thrusting his spear into its back. Taking it on his shoulders, (for he was a remarkably strong man) he lugged it along with him, and flung it down before his hungry companions. I have already hinted to you what gormandizers some of the comrades of King Ulysses were. From what is related of them, I reckon that their favorite diet was pork and that they had lived upon it until a good part of their physical substance was swine's flesh, and their tempers and dispositions were very much akin to the hog. A dish of venison, however, was no unacceptable meal to them, especially after feeding so long on oysters and clams. So, beholding the dead stag, they felt of its ribs, in a knowing way, and lost no time in kindling a fire, of driftwood, to cook it. The rest of the day was spent in feasting; and if these enormous eaters got up from table at sunset, it was only because they could not scrape another morsel off the poor animal's bones.

The next morning, their appetites were as sharp as ever. They looked at Ulysses, as if they expected him to clamber up the cliff again, and come back with another fat deer upon his shoulders. Instead of setting out, however, he summoned the whole crew together, and told them it was in vain to hope that he could kill a stag every day for their dinner, and therefore it was advisable to think of some other mode of satisfying their hunger.

"Now," said he, "when I was on the cliff yesterday, I discovered that this island is inhabited. At a considerable distance from the shore stood a marble palace, which appeared to be very spacious, and had a great deal of smoke curling out of one of its chimneys."

"Aha!" muttered some of his companions, smacking their lips. "That smoke must have come from the kitchen fire. There was a good dinner on the spit; and no doubt there will be as good a one to-day."

"But," continued the wise Ulysses, "you must remember, my good friends, our misadventure in the cavern of one-eyed Polyphemus, the Cyclops! Instead of his ordinary milk diet, did he not eat up two of our comrades for his supper, and a couple more for breakfast, and two at his supper again? Methinks I see him yet, the hideous monster, scanning us with that great red eye, in the middle of his forehead, to single out the fattest. And then, again, only a few days ago, did we not fall into the hands of the king of the Læstrygons, and those other horrible giants, his subjects, who devoured a great many more of us than are now left? To tell you the truth, if we go to yonder palace, there can be no question that we shall make our appearance at the dinner table; but whether seated as guests, or served up as food, is a point to be seriously considered."

"Either way," murmured some of the hungriest of the crew, "it will be better than starvation; particularly if one could be sure of being well fattened beforehand, and daintily cooked afterwards."

"That is a matter of taste," said King Ulysses, "and, for my own part, neither the most careful fattening nor the daintiest of cookery would reconcile me to being dished at last. My proposal is, therefore, that we divide ourselves into two equal parties, and ascertain, by drawing lots, which of the two shall go to the palace, and beg for food and assistance. If these can be obtained, all is well. If not, and if the inhabitants prove as inhospitable as Polyphemus, or the Læstrygons, then there will but half of us perish, and the remainder may set sail and escape."

As nobody objected to this scheme, Ulysses proceeded to count the whole band, and found that there were forty-six men, including himself. He then numbered off twenty-two of them, and put Eurylochus (who was one of his chief officers, and second only to himself in sagacity) at their head. Ulysses took command of the remaining twenty-two men, in person. Then, taking off his helmet, he put two shells into it, on one of which was written, "Go," and on the other, "Stay." Another person now held the helmet, while Ulysses and Eurylochus drew out each a shell; and the word "Go" was found written on that which Eurylochus had drawn. In this manner, it was decided that Ulysses and his twenty-two men were to remain at the sea-side until the other party should have found out what sort of treatment they might expect at the mysterious palace. As there was no help for it, Eurylochus immediately set forth at the head of his twenty-two followers, who went off in a very melancholy state of mind, leaving their friends in hardly better spirits than themselves.

No sooner had they clambered up the cliff, than they discerned the tall marble towers of the palace, ascending, as white as snow, out of the lovely green shadow of the trees which surrounded it. A gush of smoke came from a chimney in the rear of the edifice. This vapor rose high in the air, and, meeting with a breeze, was wafted seaward, and made to pass over the heads of the hungry mariners. When people's appetites are keen, they have a very quick scent for anything savory in the wind.

"That smoke comes from the kitchen!" cried one of them, turning up his nose as high as he could, and snuffing eagerly. "And, as sure as I'm a half-starved vagabond, I smell roast meat in it."

"Pig, roast pig!" said another. "Ah, the dainty little porker! My mouth waters for him."

"Let us make haste," cried the others, "or we shall be too late for the good cheer!"

But scarcely had they made half a dozen steps from the edge of the cliff, when a bird came fluttering to meet them. It was the same pretty little bird, with the purple wings and body, the yellow legs, the golden collar round its neck, and the crown-like tuft upon its head, whose behavior had so much surprised Ulysses. It hovered about Eurylochus, and almost brushed his face with its wings.

"Peep, peep, pe—weep!" chirped the bird.

So plaintively intelligent was the sound, that it seemed as if the little creature were going to break its heart with some mighty secret that it had to tell, and only this one poor note to tell it with.

"My pretty bird," said Eurylochus,—for he was a wary person, and let no token of harm escape his notice,—"my pretty bird, who sent you hither? And what is the message which you bring?"

"Peep, peep, pe—weep!" replied the bird, very sorrowfully.

Then it flew towards the edge of the cliff, and looked round at them, as if exceedingly anxious that they should return whence they came. Eurylochus and a few of the others were inclined to turn back. They could not help suspecting that the purple bird must be aware of something mischievous that would befall them at the palace, and the knowledge of which affected its airy spirit with a human sympathy and sorrow. But the rest of the voyagers, snuffing up the smoke from the palace kitchen, ridiculed the idea of returning to the vessel. One of them (more brutal than his fellows, and the most notorious gormandizer in the whole crew) said such a cruel and wicked thing, that I wonder the mere thought did not turn him into a wild beast in shape, as he already was in his nature.

"This troublesome and impertinent little fowl," said he, "would make a delicate titbit to begin dinner with. Just one plump morsel, melting away between the teeth. If he comes within my reach, I'll catch him, and give him to the palace cook to be roasted on a skewer."

The words were hardly out of his mouth, before the purple bird flew away, crying, "Peep, peep, pe—weep," more dolorously than ever.

"That bird," remarked Eurylochus, "knows more than we do about what awaits us at the palace."

"Come on, then," cried his comrades, "and we'll soon know as much as he does."

The party, accordingly, went onward through the green and pleasant wood. Every little while they caught new glimpses of the marble palace, which looked more and more beautiful the nearer they approached it. They soon entered a broad pathway, which seemed to be very neatly kept, and which went winding along, with streaks of sunshine falling across it, and specks of light quivering among the deepest shadows that fell from the lofty trees. It was bordered, too, with a great many sweet-smelling flowers, such as the mariners had never seen before. So rich and beautiful they were, that, if the shrubs grew wild here, and were native in the soil, then this island was surely the flower garden of the whole earth; or, if transplanted from some other clime, it must have been from the Happy Islands that lay towards the golden sunset.

"There has been a great deal of pains foolishly wasted on these flowers," observed one of the company; and I tell you what he said, that you may keep in mind what gormandizers they were. "For my part, if I were the owner of the palace, I would bid my gardener cultivate nothing but savory pot herbs to make a stuffing for roast meat, or to flavor a stew with."

"Well said!" cried the others. "But I'll warrant you there's a kitchen garden in the rear of the palace."

At one place they came to a crystal spring, and paused to drink at it for want of liquor, which they liked better. Looking into its bosom, they beheld their own faces dimly reflected, but so extravagantly distorted by the gush and motion of the water, that each of them appeared to be laughing at himself and all his companions. So ridiculous were these images of themselves, indeed, that they did really laugh aloud, and could hardly be grave again as soon as they wished. And after they had drank, they grew still merrier than before.

"It has the twang of the wine cask in it," said one, smacking his lips.

"Make haste!" cried his fellews; "we'll find the wine cask itself at the palace; and that will be better than a hundred crystal fountains."

Then they quickened their pace, and capered for joy at the thought of the savory banquet at which they hoped to be guests. But Eurylochus told them that he felt as if he were walking in a dream.

"If I am really awake," continued he, "then, in my opinion, we are on the point of meeting with some stranger adventure than any that befell us in the cave of Polyphemus, or among the gigantic man-eating Læstrygons, or in the windy palace of King Æolus, which stands on a brazen-walled island. This kind of dreamy feeling always comes over me before any wonderful occurrence. If you take my advice, you will turn back."

"No, no," answered his comrades, snuffing the air, in which the scent from the palace kitchen was now very perceptible. "We would not turn back, though we were certain that the king of the Læstrygons, as big as a mountain, would sit at the head of the table, and huge Polyphemus, the one-eyed Cyclops, at its foot."

At length they came within full sight of the palace, which proved to be very large and lofty, with a great number of airy pinnacles upon its roof. Though it was now midday, and the sun shone brightly over the marble front, yet its snowy whiteness, and its fantastic style of architecture, made it look unreal, like the frostwork on a window pane, or like the shapes of castles which one sees among the clouds by moonlight. But, just then, a puff of wind brought down the smoke of the kitchen among them, and caused each man to smell the odor of the dish that he liked best; and, after scenting it, they thought everything else moonshine, and nothing real save this palace, and save the banquet that was evidently ready to be served up in it.

So they hastened their steps towards the portal, but had not got half way across the wide lawn, when a pack of lions, tigers, and wolves came bounding to meet them. The terrified mariners started back, expecting no better fate than to be torn to pieces and devoured. To their surprise and joy, however, these wild beasts merely capered around them, wagging their tails, offering their heads to be stroked and patted, and behaving just like so many well-bred house dogs, when they wish to express their delight at meeting their master, or their master's friends. The biggest lion licked the feet of Eurylochus; and every other lion, and every wolf and tiger, singled out one of his two and twenty followers, whom the beast fondled as if he loved him better than a beef bone.

But, for all that, Eurylochus imagined that he saw something fierce and savage in their eyes; nor would he have been surprised, at any moment, to feel the big lion's terrible claws, or to see each of the tigers make a deadly spring, or each wolf leap at the throat of the man whom he had fondled. Their mildness seemed unreal, and a mere freak; but their savage nature was as true as their teeth and claws.

Nevertheless, the men went safely across the lawn with the wild beasts frisking about them, and doing no manner of harm; although, as they mounted the steps of the palace, you might possibly have heard a low growl, particularly from the wolves; as if they thought it a pity, after all, to let the strangers pass without so much as tasting what they were made of.

Eurylochus and his followers now passed under a lofty portal and looked through the open doorway into the interior of the palace. The first thing that they saw was a spacious hall and a fountain in the middle of it, gushing up towards the ceiling out of a marble basin, and falling back into it with a continual splash. The water of this fountain, as it spouted upward, was constantly taking new shapes, not very distinctly, but plainly enough for a nimble fancy to recognize what they were. Now it was the shape of a man in a long robe, the fleecy whiteness of which was made out of the fountain's spray; now it was a lion, or a tiger, or a wolf, or an ass, or, as often as anything else, a hog wallowing in the marble basin as if it were his sty. It was either magic or some very curious machinery that caused the gushing waterspout to assume all these forms. But, before the strangers had time to look closely at this wonderful sight, their attention was drawn off by a very sweet and agreeable sound. A woman's voice was singing melodiously in another room of the palace, and with her voice was mingled the noise of a loom, at which she was probably seated, weaving a rich texture of cloth, and intertwining the high and low sweetness of her voice into a rich tissue of harmony.

By and by, the song came to an end; and then, all at once, there were several feminine voices, talking airily and cheerfully, with now and then a merry burst of laughter, such as you may always hear when three or four young women sit at work together.

"What a sweet song that was!" exclaimed one of the voyagers.

"Too sweet, indeed," answered Eurylochus, shaking his head. "Yet it was not so sweet as the song of the Sirens, those bird-like damsels who wanted to tempt us on the rocks, so that our vessels might be wrecked, and our bones left whitening along the shore."

"But just listen to the pleasant voices of those maidens, and that buzz of the loom, as the shuttle passes to and fro," said another comrade. "What a domestic, household, home-like sound it is! Ah, before that weary siege of Troy, I used to hear the buzzing loom and the women's voices under my own roof. Shall I never hear them again? nor taste those nice little savory dishes which my dearest wife knew how to serve up?"

"Tush! we shall fare better here," said another. "But how innocently those women are babbling together, without guessing that we overhear them! And mark that richest voice of all, so pleasant and familiar, but which yet seems to have the authority of a mistress among them. Let us show ourselves at once. What harm can the lady of the palace and her maidens do to mariners and warriors like us?"

"Remember," said Eurylochus, "that it was a young maiden who beguiled three of our friends into the palace of the king of the Læstrygons, who ate up one of them in the twinkling of an eye."

No warning or persuasion, however, had any effect on his companions. They went up to a pair of folding doors at the farther end of the hall, and throwing them wide open, passed into the next room. Eurylochus, meanwhile, had stepped behind a pillar. In the short moment while the folding doors opened and closed again, he caught a glimpse of a very beautiful woman rising from the loom, and coming to meet the poor weather-beaten wanderers, with a hospitable smile, and her hand stretched out in welcome. There were four other young women, who joined their hands and danced merrily forward, making gestures of obeisance to the strangers. They were only less beautiful than the lady who seemed to be their mistress. Yet Eurylochus fancied that one of them had sea-green hair, and that the close-fitting bodice of a second looked like the bark of a tree, and that both the others had something odd in their aspect, although he could not quite determine what it was, in the little while that he had to examine them.

The folding doors swung quickly back, and left him standing behind the pillar, in the solitude of the outer hall. There Eurylochus waited until he was quite weary, and listened eagerly to every sound, but without hearing anything that could help him to guess what had become of his friends. Footsteps, it is true, seemed to be passing and repassing, in other parts of the palace. Then there was a clatter of silver dishes, or golden ones, which made him imagine a rich feast in a splendid banqueting hall. But by and by he heard a tremendous grunting and squealing, and then a sudden scampering, like that of small, hard hoofs over a marble floor, while the voices of the mistress and her four handmaidens were screaming all together, in tones of anger and derision. Eurylochus could not conceive what had happened, unless a drove of swine had broken into the palace, attracted by the smell of the feast. Chancing to cast his eyes at the fountain, he saw that it did not shift its shape, as formerly, nor looked either like a long-robed man, or a lion, a tiger, a wolf, or an ass. It looked like nothing but a hog, which lay wallowing in the marble basin, and filled it from brim to brim.

But we must leave the prudent Eurylochus waiting in the outer hall, and follow his friends into the inner secrecy of the palace. As soon as the beautiful woman saw them, she arose from the loom, as I have told you, and came forward, smiling, and stretching out her hand. She took the hand of the foremost among them, and bade him and the whole party welcome.

"You have been long expected, my good friends," said she. "I and my maidens are well acquainted with you, although you do not appear to recognize us. Look at this piece of tapestry, and judge if your faces must not have been familiar to us."

So the voyagers examined the web of cloth which the beautiful woman had been weaving in her loom; and, to their vast astonishment they saw their own figures perfectly represented in different colored threads. It was a lifelike picture of their recent adventures, showing them in the cave of Polyphemus, and how they had put out his one great moony eye; while in another part of the tapestry they were untying the leathern bags, puffed out with contrary winds; and farther on, they beheld themselves scampering away from the gigantic king of the Læstrygons, who had caught one of them by the leg. Lastly, there they were, sitting on the desolate shore of this very island, hungry and downcast, and looking ruefully at the bare bones of the stag which they devoured yesterday. This was as far as the work had yet proceeded; but when the beautiful woman should again sit down at her loom, she would probably make a picture of what had since happened to the strangers, and of what was now going to happen.

"You see," she said, "that I know all about your troubles; and you cannot doubt that I desire to make you happy for as long a time as you may remain with me. For this purpose, my honored guests, I have ordered a banquet prepared. Fish, fowl, and flesh, roasted, and in luscious stews, and seasoned, I trust, to all your tastes, are ready to be served up. If your appetites tell you it is dinner time, then come with me to the festal saloon."

At this kind invitation, the hungry mariners were quite overjoyed; and one of them, taking upon himself to be spokesman, assured their hospitable hostess that any hour of the day was dinner time with them, whenever they could get flesh to put in the pot, and fire to boil it with. So the beautiful woman led the way; and the four maidens, (one of them had sea-green hair, another a bodice of oak bark, a third sprinkled a shower of water drops from her fingers' ends, and the fourth had some other oddity, which I have forgotten,) all these followed behind, and hurried the guests along, until they entered a magnificent saloon. It was built in a perfect oval, and lighted from a crystal dome above. Around the walls were ranged two and twenty thrones, overhung by canopies of crimson and gold, and provided with the softest of cushions, which were tasselled and fringed with gold cord. Each of the strangers was invited to sit down; and there they were, two and twenty storm-beaten mariners, in worn and tattered garb, sitting on two and twenty cushioned and canopied thrones, so rich and gorgeous that the proudest monarch had nothing more splendid in his stateliest hall.

Then you might have seen the guests nodding, winking with one eye, and leaning from one throne to another, to communicate their satisfaction in hoarse whispers.

"Our good hostess has made kings of us all," said one. "Ha! do you smell the feast? I'll engage it will be fit to set before two and twenty kings."

"I hope," said another, "it will be, mainly, good substantial joints, surloins, spareribs, and hinder quarters, without too many kickshaws. If I thought the good lady would not take it amiss, I should call for a fat slice of fried bacon to begin with."

Ah, the gluttons and gormandizers! You see how it was with them. In the loftiest seats of dignity, on royal thrones, they could think of nothing but their greedy appetite, which was the portion of their nature that they shared with wolves and swine; so that they resembled those vilest of animals far more than they did kings—if, indeed, kings were what they ought to be.

But the beautiful woman now clapped her hands; and immediately there entered a train of two and twenty serving men bringing dishes of the richest food, all hot from the kitchen fire, and sending up such a steam that it hung like a cloud below the crystal dome of the saloon. An equal number of attendants brought great flagons of wine, of various kinds, some of which sparkled as it was poured out, and went bubbling down the throat; while, of other sorts, the purple liquor was so clear that you could see the wrought figures at the bottom of the goblet. While the servants supplied the two and twenty guests with food and drink, the hostess and her four maidens went from one throne to another, exhorting them to eat their fill, and to quaff wine abundantly, and thus to recompense themselves, at this one banquet, for the many days when they had gone without a dinner. But, whenever the mariners were not looking at them, (which was pretty often, as they looked chiefly into the basins and platters,) the beautiful woman and her damsels turned aside, and laughed. Even the servants, as they knelt down to present the dishes, might be seen to grin and sneer, while the guests were helping themselves to the offered dainties.

And, once in a while, the strangers seemed to taste something that they did not like.

"Here is an odd kind of a spice in this dish," said one. "I can't say it quite suits my palate. Down it goes, however."

"Send a good draught of wine down your throat," said his comrade on the next throne. "That is the stuff to make this sort of cookery relish well. Though I must needs say, the wine has a queer taste too. But the more I drink of it, the better I like the flavor."

Whatever little fault they might find with the dishes, they sat at dinner a prodigiously long while; and it would really have made you ashamed to see how they swilled down the liquor and gobbled up the food. They sat on golden thrones, to be sure; but they behaved like pigs in a sty; and, if they had their wits about them, they might have guessed that this was the opinion of their beautiful hostess and her maidens. It brings a blush into my face to reckon up, in my own mind, what mountains of meat and pudding, and what gallons of wine, these two and twenty guzzlers and gormandizers ate and drank. They forgot all about their homes, and their wives and children, and all about Ulysses, and everything else, except this banquet, at which they wanted to keep feasting forever. But at length they began to give over, from mere incapacity to hold any more.

"That last bit of fat is too much for me," said one.

"And I have not room for another morsel," said his next neighbor, heaving a sigh. "What a pity! My appetite is as sharp as ever."

In short, they all left off eating, and leaned back on their thrones, with such a stupid and helpless aspect as made them ridiculous to behold. When their hostess saw this, she laughed aloud; so did her four damsels; so did the two and twenty serving men that bore the dishes, and their two and twenty fellows that poured out the wine. And the louder they all laughed, the more stupid and helpless did the two and twenty gormandizers look. Then the beautiful woman took her stand in the middle of the saloon, and stretching out a slender rod, (it had been all the while in her hand, although they never noticed it till this moment,) she turned it from one guest to another, until each had felt it pointed at himself. Beautiful as her face was, and though there was a smile on it, it looked just as wicked and mischievous as the ugliest serpent that ever was seen; and fat-witted as the voyagers had made themselves, they began to suspect that they had fallen into the power of an evil-minded enchantress.

"Wretches," cried she, "you have abused a lady's hospitality; and in this princely saloon your behavior has been suited to a hogpen. You are already swine in everything but the human form, which you disgrace, and which I myself should be ashamed to keep a moment longer, were you to share it with me. But it will require only the slightest exercise of magic to make the exterior conform to the hoggish disposition. Assume your proper shapes, gormandizers, and begone to the sty!"

Uttering these last words, she waved her wand; and stamping her foot imperiously, each of the guests was struck aghast at beholding, instead of his comrades in human shape, one and twenty hogs sitting on the same number of golden thrones. Each man (as he still supposed himself to be) essayed to give a cry of surprise, but found that he could merely grunt, and that, in a word, he was just such another beast as his companions. It looked so intolerably absurd to see hogs on cushioned thrones, that they made haste to wallow down upon all fours, like other swine. They tried to groan and beg for mercy, but forthwith emitted the most awful grunting and squealing that ever came out of swinish throats. They would have wrung their hands in despair, but, attempting to do so, grew all the more desperate for seeing themselves squatted on their hams, and pawing the air with their fore trotters. Dear me! what pendulous ears they had! what little red eyes, half buried in fat! and what long snouts, instead of Grecian noses!

But brutes as they certainly were, they yet had enough of human nature in them to be shocked at their own hideousness; and, still intending to groan, they uttered a viler grunt and squeal than before. So harsh and ear-piercing it was, that you would have fancied a butcher was sticking his knife into each of their throats, or, at the very least, that somebody was pulling every hog by his funny little twist of a tail.

"Begone to your sty!" cried the enchantress, giving them some smart strokes with her wand; and then she turned to the serving men—"Drive out these swine, and throw down some acorns for them to eat."

The door of the saloon being flung open, the drove of hogs ran in all directions save the right one, in accordance with their hoggish perversity but were finally driven into the back yard of the palace. It was a sight to bring tears into one's eyes, (and I hope none of you will be cruel enough to laugh at it,) to see the poor creatures go snuffing along, picking up here a cabbage leaf and there a turnip top, and rooting their noses in the earth for whatever they could find. In their sty, moreover, they behaved more piggishly than the pigs that had been born so; for they bit and snorted at one another, put their feet in the trough, and gobbled up their victuals in a ridiculous hurry; and, when there was nothing more to be had, they made a great pile of themselves among some unclean straw, and fell fast asleep. If they had any human reason left, it was just enough to keep them wondering when they should be slaughtered, and what quality of bacon they should make.

Meantime, as I told you before, Eurylochus had waited, and waited, and waited, in the entrance hall of the palace, without being able to comprehend what had befallen his friends. At last, when the swinish uproar resounded through the palace, and when he saw the image of a hog in the marble basin, he thought it best to hasten back to the vessel, and inform the wise Ulysses of these marvellous occurrences. So he ran as fast as he could down the steps, and never stopped to draw breath till he reached the shore.

"Why do you come alone?" asked King Ulysses, as soon as he saw him.

"Where are your two and twenty comrades?"

At these questions, Eurylochus burst into tears.

"Alas!" cried he, "I greatly fear that we shall never see one of their faces again."

Then he told Ulysses all that had happened, as far as he knew it, and added that he suspected the beautiful woman to be a vile enchantress, and the marble palace, magnificent as it looked, to be only a dismal cavern in reality. As for his companions, he could not imagine what had become of them, unless they had been given to the swine to be devoured alive. At this intelligence, all the voyagers were greatly affrighted. But Ulysses lost no time in girding on his sword, and hanging his bow and quiver over his shoulders, and taking a spear in his right hand. When his followers saw their wise leader making these preparations, they inquired whither he was going, and earnestly besought him not to leave them.

"You are our king," cried they; "and what is more, you are the wisest man in the whole world, and nothing but your wisdom and courage can get us out of this danger. If you desert us, and go to the enchanted palace, you will suffer the same fate as our poor companions, and not a soul of us will ever see our dear Ithaca again."

"As I am your king," answered Ulysses, "and wiser than any of you, it is therefore the more my duty to see what has befallen our comrades, and whether anything can yet be done to rescue them. Wait for me here until to-morrow. If I do not then return, you must hoist sail, and endeavor to find your way to our native land. For my part, I am answerable for the fate of these poor mariners, who have stood by my side in battle, and been so often drenched to the skin, along with me, by the same tempestuous surges. I will either bring them back with me, or perish."

Had his followers dared, they would have detained him by force. But King Ulysses frowned sternly on them, and shook his spear, and bade them stop him at their peril. Seeing him so determined, they let him go, and sat down on the sand, as disconsolate a set of people as could be, waiting and praying for his return.

It happened to Ulysses, just as before, that, when he had gone a few steps from the edge of the cliff, the purple bird came fluttering towards him, crying, "Peep, peep, pe—weep!" and using all the art it could to persuade him to go no farther.

"What mean you, little bird?" cried Ulysses. "You are arrayed like a king in purple and gold, and wear a golden crown upon your head. Is it because I too am a king, that you desire so earnestly to speak with me? If you can talk in human language, say what you would have me do."

"Peep!" answered the purple bird, very dolorously. "Peep, peep, pe—we—ep!"

Certainly there lay some heavy anguish at the little bird's heart; and it was a sorrowful predicament that he could not, at least, have the consolation of telling what it was. But Ulysses had no time to waste in trying to get at the mystery. He therefore quickened his pace, and had gone a good way along the pleasant wood path when there met him a young man of very brisk and intelligent aspect, and clad in a rather singular garb. He wore a short cloak, and a sort of cap that seemed to be furnished with a pair of wings; and from the lightness of his step, you would have supposed that there might likewise be wings on his feet. To enable him to walk still better, (for he was always on one journey or another,) he carried a winged staff, around which two serpents were wriggling and twisting. In short, I have said enough to make you guess that it was Quicksilver; and Ulysses (who knew him of old, and had learned a great deal of his wisdom from him) recognized him in a moment.

"Whither are you going in such a hurry, wise Ulysses?" asked Quicksilver. "Do you not know that this island is enchanted? The wicked enchantress (whose name is Circe, the sister of King Æetes) dwells in the marble palace which you see yonder among the trees. By her magic arts, she changes every human being into the brute beast or fowl whom he happens most to resemble."

"That little bird, which met me at the edge of the cliff," exclaimed Ulysses; "was he a human being once?"

"Yes," answered Quicksilver. "He was once a king, named Picus, and a pretty good sort of a king too, only rather too proud of his purple robe, and his crown, and the golden chain about his neck; so he was forced to take the shape of a gaudy-feathered bird. The lions, and wolves, and tigers, who will come running to meet you, in front of the palace, were formerly fierce and cruel men, resembling in their dispositions the wild beasts whose forms they now rightfully wear."

"And my poor companions," said Ulysses. "Have they undergone a similar change, through the arts of this wicked Circe?"

"You well know what gormandizers they were," replied Quicksilver; and rogue that he was, he could not help laughing at the joke. "So you will not be surprised to hear that they have all taken the shapes of swine! If Circe had never done anything worse, I really should not think her so very much to blame."

"But can I do nothing to help them?" inquired Ulysses.

"It will require all your wisdom," said Quicksilver, "and a little of my own into the bargain, to keep your royal and sagacious self from being transformed into a fox. But do as I bid you, and the matter may end better than it has begun."

While he was speaking, Quicksilver seemed to be in search of something; he went stooping along the ground, and soon laid his hand on a little plant with a snow-white flower, which he plucked and smelt of. Ulysses had been looking at that very spot only just before; and it appeared to him that the plant had burst into full flower the instant when Quicksilver touched it with his fingers.

"Take this flower, King Ulysses," said he. "Guard it as you do your eyesight; for I can assure you it is exceedingly rare and precious, and you might seek the whole earth over without ever finding another like it. Keep it in your hand, and smell of it frequently after you enter the palace, and while you are talking with the enchantress. Especially when she offers you food, or a draught of wine out of her goblet, be careful to fill your nostrils with the flower's fragrance. Follow these directions, and you may defy her magic arts to change you into a fox."

Quicksilver then gave him some further advice how to behave, and bidding him to be bold and prudent, again assured him that, powerful as Circe was, he would have a fair prospect of coming safely out of her enchanted palace. After listening attentively, Ulysses thanked his good friend, and resumed his way. But he had taken only a few steps, when, recollecting some other questions which he wished to ask, he turned round again, and beheld nobody on the spot where Quicksilver had stood; for that winged cap of his, and those winged shoes, with the help of the winged staff, had carried him quickly out of sight.

When Ulysses reached the lawn, in front of the palace, the lions and other savage animals came bounding to meet him, and would have fawned upon him and licked his feet. But the wise king struck at them with his long spear, and sternly bade them begone out of his path; for he knew that they had once been bloodthirsty men, and would now tear him limb from limb, instead of fawning upon him, could they do the mischief that was in their hearts. The wild beasts yelped and glared at him, and stood at a distance, while he ascended the palace steps.

On entering the hall, Ulysses saw the magic fountain in the center of it. The up-gushing water had now again taken the shape of a man in a long, white, fleecy robe, who appeared to be making gestures of welcome. The king likewise heard the noise of the shuttle in the loom, and the sweet melody of the beautiful woman's song, and then the pleasant voices of herself and the four maidens talking together, with peals of merry laughter intermixed. But

Ulysses did not waste much time in listening to the laughter or the song. He leaned his spear against one of the pillars of the hall, and then, after loosening his sword in the scabbard, stepped boldly forward, and threw the folding doors wide open. The moment she beheld his stately figure standing in the doorway, the beautiful woman rose from the loom, and ran to meet him with a glad smile throwing its sunshine over her face, and both her hands extended.

"Welcome, brave stranger!" cried she. "We were expecting you."

And the nymph with the sea-green hair made a courtesy down to the ground, and likewise bade him welcome; so did her sister with the bodice of oaken bark, and she that sprinkled dewdrops from her fingers' ends, and the fourth one with some oddity which I cannot remember. And Circe, as the beautiful enchantress was called, (who had deluded so many persons that she did not doubt of being able to delude Ulysses, not imagining how wise he was,) again addressed him:—

"Your companions," said she, "have already been received into my palace, and have enjoyed the hospitable treatment to which the propriety of their behavior so well entitles them. If such be your pleasure, you shall first take some refreshment, and then join them in the elegant apartment which they now occupy. See, I and my maidens have been weaving their figures into this piece of tapestry."

She pointed to the web of beautifully-woven cloth in the loom. Circe and the four nymphs must have been very diligently at work since the arrival of the mariners; for a great many yards of tapestry had now been wrought, in addition to what I before described. In this new part, Ulysses saw his two and twenty friends represented as sitting on cushioned and canopied thrones, greedily devouring dainties, and quaffing deep draughts of wine. The work had not yet gone any further. O, no, indeed. The enchantress was far too cunning to let Ulysses see the mischief which her magic arts had since brought upon the gormandizers.

"As for yourself, valiant sir," said Circe, "judging by the dignity of your aspect, I take you to be nothing less than a king. Deign to follow me, and you shall be treated as befits your rank."

So Ulysses followed her into the oval saloon, where his two and twenty comrades had devoured the banquet, which ended so disastrously for themselves. But, all this while, he had held the snow-white flower in his hand, and had constantly smelt of it while Circe was speaking; and as he crossed the threshold of the saloon, he took good care to inhale several long and deep snuffs of its fragrance. Instead of two and twenty thrones, which had before been ranged around the wall, there was now only a single throne, in the center of the apartment. But this was surely the most magnificent seat that ever a king or an emperor reposed himself upon, all made of chased gold, studded with precious stones, with a cushion that looked like a soft heap of living roses, and overhung by a canopy of sunlight which Circe knew how to weave into drapery. The enchantress took Ulysses by the hand, and made him sit down upon this dazzling throne. Then, clapping her hands, she summoned the chief butler.

"Bring hither," said she, "the goblet that is set apart for kings to drink out of. And fill it with the same delicious wine which my royal brother King Æetes praised so highly, when he last visited me with my fair daughter Medea. That good and amiable child! Were she now here, it would delight her to see me offering this wine to my honored guest."

But Ulysses, while the butler was gone for the wine, held the snow-white flower to his nose.

"Is it a wholesome wine?" he asked.

At this the four maidens tittered; whereupon the enchantress looked around at them, with an aspect of severity.

"It is the wholesomest juice that ever was squeezed out of the grape," said she; "for, instead of disguising a man, as other liquor is apt to do, it brings him to his true self, and shows him as he ought to be."

The chief butler liked nothing better than to see people turned into swine, or making any kind of a beast of themselves; so he made haste to bring the royal goblet, filled with a liquid as bright as gold, and which kept sparkling upward, and throwing a sunny spray over the brim. But, delightfully as the wine looked, it was mingled with the most potent enchantments that Circe knew how to concoct. For every drop of the pure grape juice there were two drops of the pure mischief; and the danger of the thing was, that the mischief made it taste all the better. The mere smell of the bubbles, which effervesced at the brim, was enough to turn a man's beard into pig's bristles, or make a lion's claws grow out of his fingers, or a fox's brush behind him.

"Drink, my noble guest," said Circe, smiling as she presented him with the goblet. "You will find in this draught a solace for all your troubles."

King Ulysses took the goblet with his right hand, while with his left he held the snow-white flower to his nostrils, and drew in so long a breath that his lungs were quite filled with its pure and simple fragrance. Then, drinking off all the wine, he looked the enchantress calmly in the face.

"Wretch," cried Circe, giving him a smart stroke with her wand, "how dare you keep your human shape a moment longer? Take the form of the brute whom you most resemble. If a hog, go join your fellow-swine in the sty; if a lion, a wolf, a tiger, go howl with the wild beasts on the lawn; if a fox, go exercise your craft in stealing poultry. Thou hast quaffed off my wine, and canst be man no longer."

But, such was the virtue of the snow-white flower, instead of wallowing down from his throne in swinish shape, or taking any other brutal form, Ulysses looked even more manly and king-like than before. He gave the magic goblet a toss, and sent it clashing over the marble floor, to the farthest end of the saloon. Then drawing his sword, he seized the enchantress by her beautiful ringlets, and made a gesture as if he meant to strike off her head at one blow.

"Wicked Circe," cried he in a terrible voice, "this sword shall put an end to thy enchantments. Thou shalt die, vile witch, and do no more mischief in the world, by tempting human beings into the vices which make beasts of them."

The tone and countenance of Ulysses were so awful, and his sword gleamed so brightly, and seemed to have so intolerably keen an edge, that Circe was almost killed by the mere fright, without waiting for the blow. The chief butler scrambled out of the saloon, picking up the golden goblet as he went; and the enchantress and the four maidens fell on their knees, wringing their hands, and screaming for mercy.

"Spare me!" cried Circe. "Spare me, royal and wise Ulysses. For now I know that thou art he of whom Quicksilver forewarned me, the most prudent of mortals, against whom no enchantments can prevail. Thou only couldst have conquered Circe. Spare me, wisest of men. I will show thee true hospitality, and even give myself to be thy slave, and this magnificent palace to be henceforth thy home."

The four nymphs, meanwhile, were making a most piteous ado; and especially the ocean nymph, with the sea-green hair, wept a great deal of salt water, and the fountain nymph, besides scattering dewdrops from her fingers' ends, nearly melted away into tears. But Ulysses would not be pacified until Circe had taken a solemn oath to change back his companions, and as many others as he should direct, from their present forms of beast or bird into their former shapes of men.

"On these conditions" said he, "I consent to spare your life. Otherwise you must die on the spot."

With a drawn sword hanging over her, the enchantress would readily have consented to do as much good as she had hitherto done mischief, however little she might like such employment. She therefore led Ulysses out of the back entrance of the palace, and showed him the swine in their sty. There were about fifty of these unclean beasts in the whole herd; and though the greater part were hogs by birth and education, there was wonderfully little difference to be seen betwixt them and their new brethren who had so recently worn the human shape. To speak critically, indeed, the latter rather carried the thing to excess, and seemed to make it a point to wallow in the miriest part of the sty, and otherwise to outdo the original swine in their own natural vocation. When men once turn to brutes, the trifle of man's wit that remains in them adds tenfold to their brutality.

The comrades of Ulysses, however, had not quite lost the remembrance of having formerly stood erect. When he approached the sty, two and twenty enormous swine separated themselves from the herd, and scampered towards him, with such a chorus of horrible squealing as made him clap both hands to his ears. And yet they did not seem to know what they wanted, nor whether they were merely hungry, or miserable from some other cause. It was curious, in the midst of their distress, to observe them thrusting their noses into the mire, in quest of something to eat. The nymph with the bodice of oaken bark (she was the hamadryad of an oak) threw a handful of acorns among them; and the two and twenty hogs scrambled and fought for the prize, as if they had tasted not so much as a noggin of sour milk for a twelvemonth.

"These must certainly be my comrades," said Ulysses. "I recognize their dispositions. They are hardly worth the trouble of changing them into the human form again. Nevertheless, we will have it done, lest their bad example should corrupt the other hogs. Let them take their original shapes, therefore, Dame Circe, if your skill is equal to the task. It will require greater magic, I trow, than it did to make swine of them."

So Circe waved her wand again, and repeated a few magic words, at the sound of which the two and twenty hogs pricked up their pendulous ears. It was a wonder to behold how their snouts grew shorter and shorter, and their mouths (which they seemed to be sorry for, because they could not gobble so expeditiously) smaller and smaller, and how one and another began to stand upon his hind legs, and scratch his nose with his fore trotters. At first the spectators hardly knew whether to call them hogs or men, but by and by came to the conclusion that they rather resembled the latter. Finally, there stood the twenty-two comrades of Ulysses, looking pretty much the same as when they left the vessel.

You must not imagine, however, that the swinish quality had entirely gone out of them. When once it fastens itself into a person's character, it is very difficult getting rid of it. This was proved by the hamadryad, who, being exceedingly fond of mischief, threw another handful of acorns before the twenty-two newly restored people; whereupon down they wallowed, in a moment, and gobbled them up in a very shameful way. Then, recollecting themselves, they scrambled to their feet, and looked more than commonly foolish.

"Thanks, noble Ulysses!" they cried. "From brute beasts you have restored us to the condition of men again."

"Do not put yourselves to the trouble of thanking me," said the wise king. "I fear I have done but little for you."

To say the truth, there was a suspicious kind of a grunt in their voices, and, for a long time afterwards, they spoke gruffly, and were apt to set up a squeal.

"It must depend on your own future behavior," added Ulysses, "whether you do not find your way back to the sty."

At this moment, the note of a bird sounded from the branch of a neighboring tree.

"Peep, peep, pe—wee—ep!"

It was the purple bird, who, all this while, had been sitting over their heads, watching what was going forward, and hoping that Ulysses would remember how he had done his utmost to keep him and his followers out of harm's way. Ulysses ordered Circe instantly to make a king of this good little fowl and leave him exactly as she had found him. Hardly were the words spoken and before the bird had time to utter another "pe—weep," King Picus leaped down from the bough of the tree, as majestic a sovereign as any in the world, dressed in a long purple robe and gorgeous yellow stockings, with a splendidly wrought collar about his neck, and a golden crown upon his head. He and King Ulysses exchanged with one another the courtesies which belonged to their elevated rank. But from that time forth, King Picus was no longer proud of his crown and his trappings of royalty nor of the fact of his being a king; he felt himself merely the upper servant of his people, and that it must be his lifelong labor to make them better and happier.

As for the lions, tigers, and wolves, (though Circe would have restored them to their former shapes at his slightest word,) Ulysses thought it advisable that they should remain as they now were, and thus give warning of their cruel dispositions, instead of going about under the guise of men, and pretending to human sympathies, while their hearts had the bloodthirstiness of wild beasts. So he let them howl as much as they liked, but never troubled his head about them. And, when everything was settled according to his pleasure, he sent to summon the remainder of his comrades, whom he had left at the sea shore. These being arrived, with the prudent Eurylochus at their head, they all made themselves comfortable in Circe's enchanted palace, until quite rested and refreshed from the toils and hardships of their voyage.

9 791041 821075